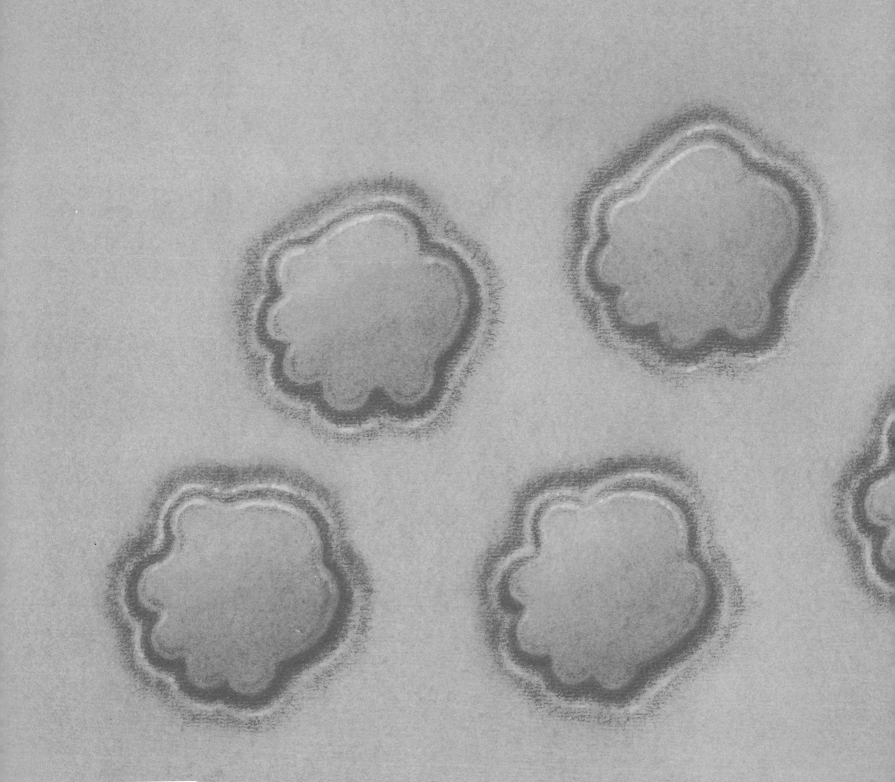

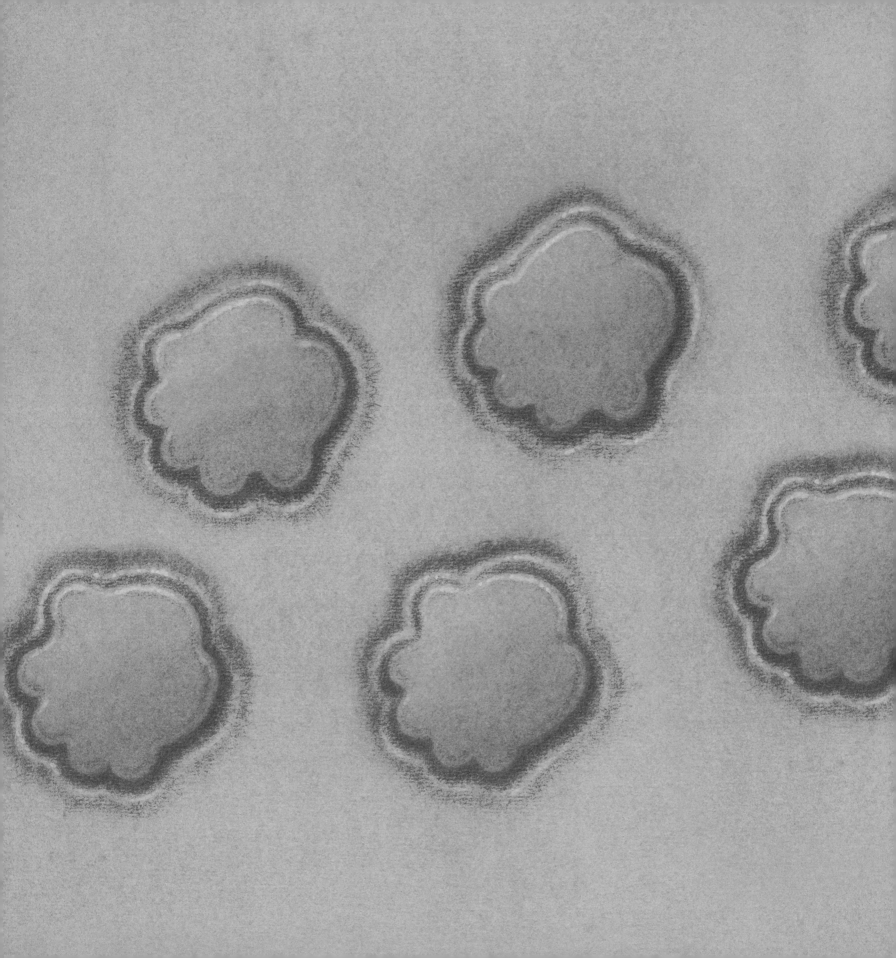

THIS BOOK IS FOR:

_____

WITH LOTS OF LOVE FROM:

_____

ON THIS DATE:

_____

"To Cindy, my love."

ZONDERKIDZ

Fiona, Love at the Zoo
Copyright © 2022 by Zondervan
Illustrations © 2022 by Zondervan

Requests for information
should be addressed to:

Zonderkidz, 3900 Sparks Dr. SE,
Grand Rapids, Michigan 49546

Hardcover ISBN 978-0-310-77085-5
Ebook ISBN 978-0-310-77086-2

Library of Congress Cataloging-in-Publication Data

Names: Cowdrey, Richard, illustrator.
Title: Fiona, love at the zoo / illustrated by Richard Cowdrey.
Description: Grand Rapids, Michigan : Zonderkidz, [2022] | Series: A Fiona
   the hippo book | Audience: Ages 4-8. | Summary: Fiona the hippo visits
   her zoo friends and discovers how different animals show their affection
   and love.
Identifiers: LCCN 2022003349 (print) | LCCN 2022003350 (ebook) | ISBN
   9780310770855 (hardcover) | ISBN 9780310770862 (ebook)
Subjects: CYAC: Love--Fiction. | Fiona (Hippopotamus), 2017---Fiction. |
   Hippopotamus--Fiction. | Zoo animals--Fiction. | LCGFT: Animal fiction.
   | Picture books.
Classification: LCC PZ8.3 .F6264 2022 (print) | LCC PZ8.3 (ebook) | DDC
   [E]--dc23
LC record available at https://lccn.loc.gov/2022003349

LC ebook record available at https://lccn.loc.gov/2022003350

Any internet addresses (websites, blogs, etc.) and telephone numbers in this book are
offered as a resource. They are not intended in any way to be or imply an endorsement
by Zondervan, nor does Zondervan vouch for the content of these sites and numbers
for the life of this book.

Illustrated by: Richard Cowdrey
Contributors: Barbara Herndon and Mary Hassinger
Art direction and design: Cindy Davis

Printed in Malaysia

22 23 24 25 /IMG/ 20 19 18 17 16 15 14 13 12 11 10 9 8 7 6 5 4 3 2 1

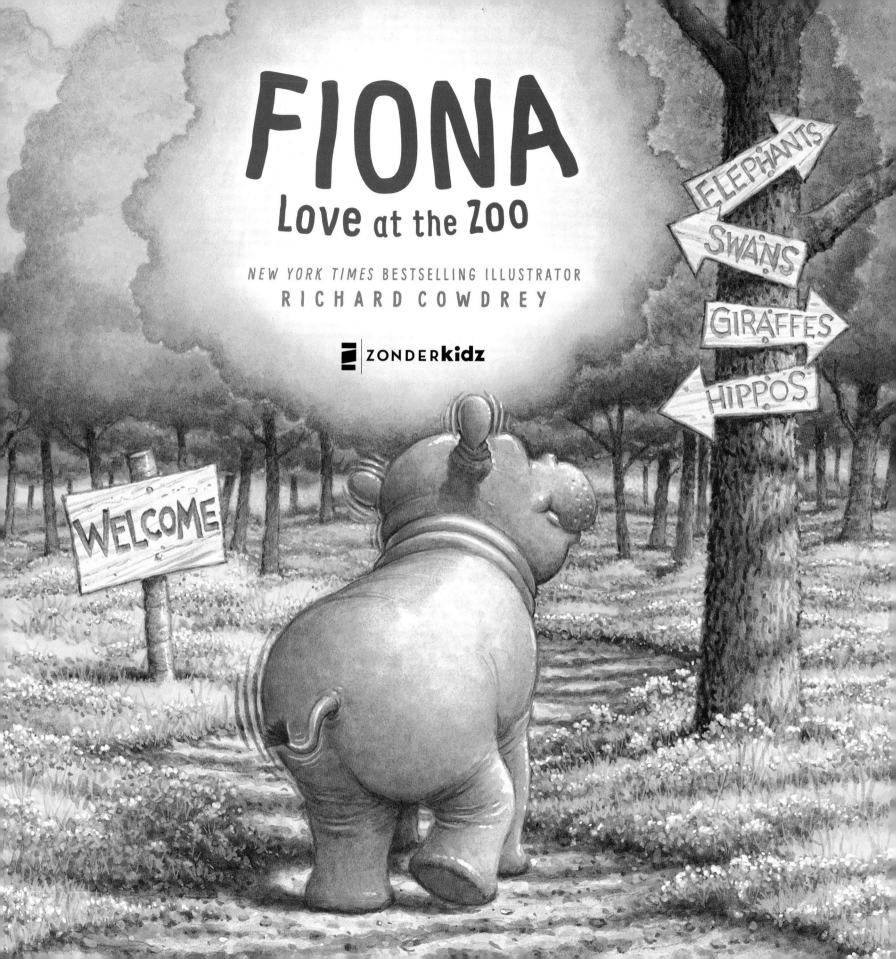

FIONA
Love at the ZOO

NEW YORK TIMES BESTSELLING ILLUSTRATOR
RICHARD COWDREY

ZONDER**kidz**

WELCOME

ELEPHANTS
SWANS
GIRAFFES
HIPPOS

Love is all around the zoo.
While critters show how much they care,
Fiona sees love everywhere!

Look way up! What do you see?
Giraffes are peeking through the tree.
Neck-in-neck, safe and snug—
you're never too tall for a hug.

Monkeys are a silly bunch
and show their love by sharing lunch.
Hugs and kisses happen, too,
while mama grooms her hairy crew.

Swans will do a water dance
to try and spark a new romance.
Side-by-side they float and glide
to show us how they feel inside.

Elephants will lean in close
with the ones they love the most.
Sweet cuddles and a gentle touch
say, "I love you very much."

These two are a prickly pair
but show us love is in the air.
Gently touching nose to nose,
these porcupines' affection shows.

Mama Wallaby jumps for joy
while cradling her baby boy.
In her pouch, he's safe and sound.
This baby knows where love is found.

Warthogs have a funny name,
but love their family all the same.
They like to keep their loved ones near,
grunting sweetly in their ear.

Look, there's mama, sister, brother,
cuddled up with one another.
This is love, red panda style,
as family snuggles for a while.

Seals are known for booping noses.

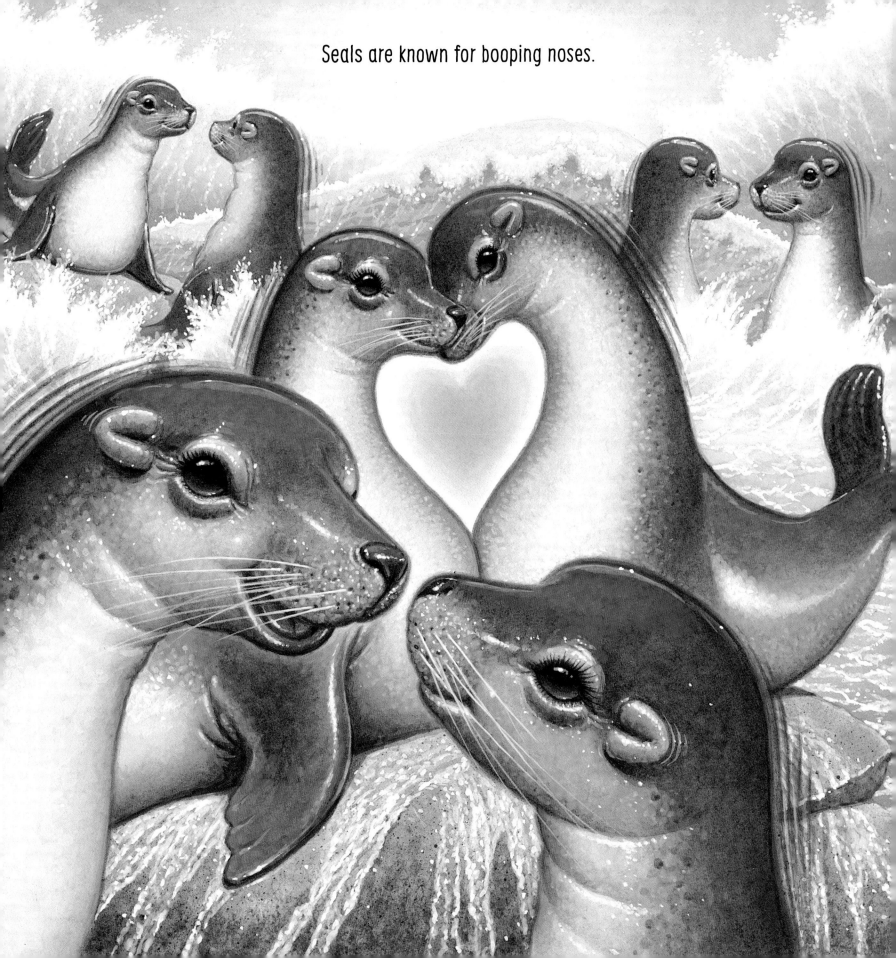

Peacocks strike dramatic poses.

Bears and cubs—they love to wrestle.

Chilly penguins peck and nestle.

Now look up! What do you see?
Two lovebirds perched up in a tree.
They sweetly rub their beaks together,
knowing love will last forever.

Love is all around the zoo.
No matter where Fiona roams ...

Her favorite love is back at home.

Snuggled under stars above,
Fiona feels BIG hippo love.

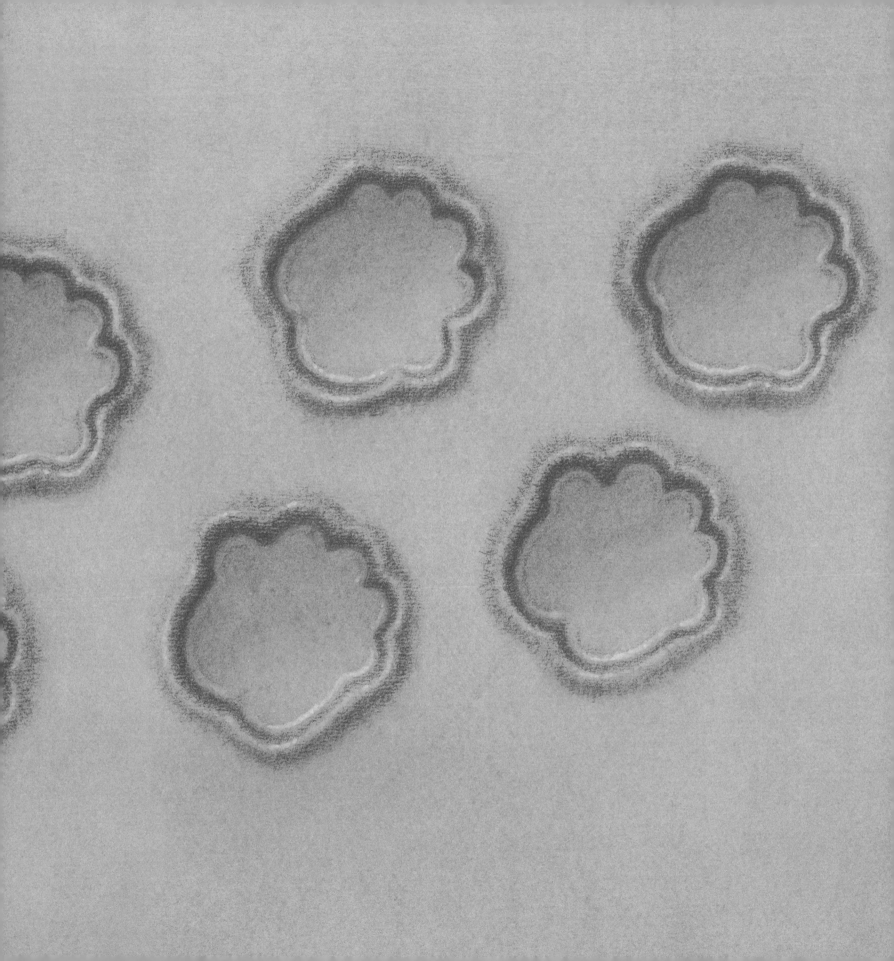

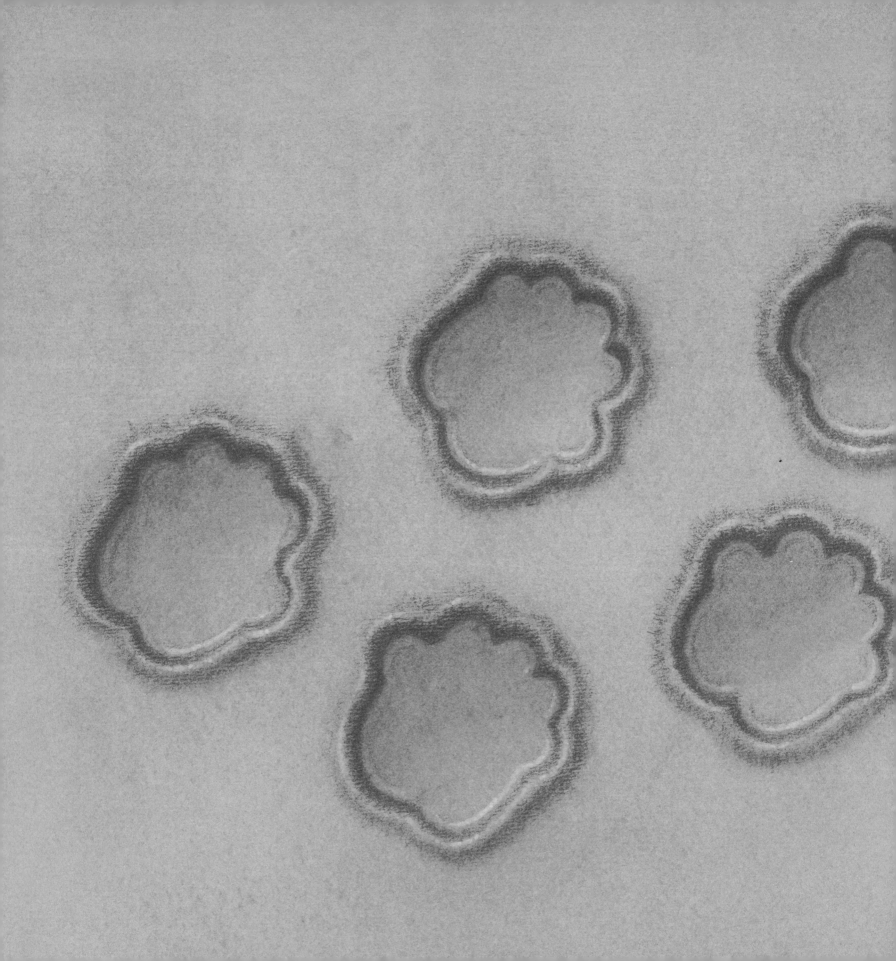